KU-739-844

Enid Blyton's
TELL-A-STORY BOOK

Andrew's Robin
and other stories

The Poor Little Sparrow

EVERY morning Ronnie and Sylvia put out crumbs for the birds, and a little bowl of water. The birds always knew when the children were going to throw out the food, and they came flocking down to wait.

"Chirrup-chirrup!" said all the sparrows, dressed in brown.

"Tirry-lee, tirry-lee!" sang the robin in his creamy voice.

"Fizz, splutter, wheeee!" chattered the starlings in their funny voices.

"Pink, pink!" shouted the pink-chested chaffinch.

"Aren't they lovely?" said the children, as they threw out the crumbs and some crusts from the toast. "They really are friendly little things."

The children knew all the birds, though it was difficult to tell one sparrow from another. They knew the smallest one of all, though, because he had one white feather in his tail, and that made him look rather queer.

One day the little sparrow flew down with the others, but it couldn't seem to stand on the ground properly. It fell over—then tried to stand upright again—and then fell over again.

"Look at the poor little sparrow," said Sylvia, who was very tender-hearted. "What's the matter with it? It can't stand."

"It's hurt its leg," said Ronnie. "Oh, Sylvia—I believe its leg is broken. Can you see?"

Sylvia went slowly closer to the birds. They did not mind, for they trusted the two children. "Oh, Ronnie, you are right," she said. "It's leg is broken in two. Whatever are we to do?"

Now the poor little sparrow had that morning been caught by a cat, but had managed to get away. Its little leg had been broken, and the tiny creature did not know why it could not stand properly, nor why it was in pain. It had joined the other birds as usual for its breakfast, but it could not eat, for it felt too ill.

Suddenly it fell right over and lay on the grass. Its eyes closed. Sylvia picked it up gently and put its soft little head against her cheek.

"Poor little sparrow," she said. "It says in the Bible that God sees every sparrow that falls, so I expect He saw you too, and hoped I would pick you up. Well, I have—but I don't know what to do to make you better."

But Mother knew. As soon as she saw the little

bird she took out the old, empty, canary's cage and put the sparrow on to some clean sand at the bottom of the cage.

"It has had a shock," said Mother. "It will come awake presently, and will be all right. Oh, look! Its leg is broken!"

"How can we mend it?" asked Sylvia, almost in tears.

"Well," said Mother, "if we break our legs the doctor sets the bone in the right position, and then ties it to something that will keep it straight till the broken bone joins together and grows properly again. What can we tie to the sparrow's tiny leg to keep it straight?"

"A match—a match!" cried Ronnie, and he emptied some out of a box.

"That's a good idea," said Mother. She gently picked up the sparrow, whose eyes were still closed, and laid it on the table. Then she tried to set the poor little leg straight. With strands of silk she fastened the straight matchstick to the thin, small leg. It looked very queer—but now the broken leg was straight again.

"Oh, Mother," said Sylvia joyfully, "you've done it so nicely. When the bone joins again, the leg will be quite all right, won't it?"

"I hope so," said Mother, putting the sparrow into the cage and shutting the door. "We shall keep the tiny thing in here, and feed it until the leg is quite right, and then it shall go free again."

When the sparrow opened its eyes it was surprised to find itself in a cage. Its leg still felt strange, but it now no longer fell over, because the matchstick supported it. The little bird flew to a perch and chirruped.

Ronnie gave it some seed. Sylvia gave it a mixture of potato and breadcrumbs, and the sparrow was simply delighted. It had a little dish of water for a bath and another dish to drink from, set at the side of the big cage. At first it fluttered its wings against the bars of the cage to get out, for it hated not being free. But, as it still did not feel very well it soon gave up struggling and sat contentedly on a perch, feeding and bathing whenever it wanted to.

The leg healed quickly. It was marvellous to see it. The skin joined nicely, and the broken bones seemed to grow together at once.

"I think we might let our little sparrow fly away now," said Mother one day. "I am sure his leg is all right."

"Are you going to take the matchstick off now?" asked Sylvia.

"Yes," said Mother. So she took hold of the half-frightened bird, and carefully and gently took away the silk binding from the leg and match. The match fell off—and the little leg was as straight and strong as ever.

"We've mended its leg! We've mended its leg!" shouted the children in delight. "You aren't a poor little sparrow any more. Fly away, fly away!"

The sparrow gave a chirrup and flew straight out of the window. How glad it was to be out of the cage! It flew into the trees, and chirruped so loudly that all the other sparrows came round to hear what it had to say.

Now you would not think that a small sparrow could possibly help the children in anything, would you? And yet, a few weeks later, a very strange thing happened.

Ronnie and Sylvia had some glass marbles, the prettiest things you ever saw. They were blue and green and pink, and had queer white lines curving through them. Ronnie and Sylvia were very proud of them, for they had belonged to their Daddy.

"You can't get marbles like these nowadays," said Daddy. "Take care of them."

Well, Ronnie and Sylvia took them to play with in the fields, and there they met David, a big rough boy whom none of the children liked. When he saw the marbles he came up.

"Give me those," he said, "and I'll give you these reins of mine."

"No, thank you," said Ronnie, gathering his marbles up quickly. But he wasn't quick enough. David grabbed some of them and ran off laughing. Sylvia and Ronnie went after him.

"They are *our* marbles!" shouted Ronnie. "Give them back, David!"

"I'll put them somewhere and you take them," called back David—and what do you suppose he did with them? Why, the horrid boy dropped them all into a hole in a tree. Then he ran off, giggling.

Ronnie and Sylvia ran to the tree. They tried to slip their small hands into the hole but they couldn't. The hole was too small.

"We can't get our marbles out," said Sylvia. "They're gone. Oh, that horrid boy!"

"Chirrup!" said a cheerful little voice near by. The children looked up. It was their little sparrow. They knew it was the same one because of the white feather in his tail.

"I wish *you* could get our marbles," sighed Ronnie. "Your foot is quite small enough to go into the hole, sparrow."

"Chirrup!" said the sparrow—and what do you think he did? Why, he flew to the hole, and instead of putting in his foot, he put the whole of himself in. Yes, he quite disappeared into that little hole—but not for long.

He popped up again, head-first—and in his beak he held a green marble. He dropped it on to the ground and disappeared into the hole once more. Up he came, with a blue marble this time. The children were so astonished that they didn't even pick up the marbles.

The little sparrow fetched every single marble out of the hole before he flew off with a last cheerful chirrup. Then the children picked them up, and went racing home to tell Mother the strange and lovely happening.

"How very extraordinary!" said Mother. "It must be put into a story, for everyone will love to read about the poor little sparrow that did such a kind thing. It just shows what friends we can make, if only we are kind to even the smallest things."

So here is the story—and I do hope you enjoyed it, and will know what to do if *you* come across a bird with a little broken leg.

The Dormouse
and the Fairy

ONCE upon a time there was a little fat dormouse with a soft coat and a woffly nose. He was looking for a good place to go to sleep in for the cold days of winter—and at last he found one.

It wasn't really a very good place, but the dormouse didn't know that. It was in a greenhouse, inside a plant-pot that was turned on its side. A few dead leaves had blown inside, and it felt warm and cosy there. The dormouse sniffed round a bit and decided that it would be a splendid place for a winter's sleep.

So into the pot he crept, covered himself up with the leaves, put his nose between his front paws, and went to sleep.

The frost came, but it didn't get inside the plant-pot. The snow came, but there was none in the old greenhouse. The little dormouse might have slept there all winter if the gardener hadn't suddenly thought of painting the house inside and out.

Before he painted it he tidied it. He took all the

pots and saucers and cleaned them. He set them up in rows—and then, as he worked, he came to the one where the little dormouse slept.

He took it up—and he saw the dormouse inside.

"A dozymouse," he said. "Well, I never! Are you the little rascal that nibbles my plants in the spring?"

He shook out the little dormouse, and the poor, sleepy little thing woke up with a dreadful jump! Somehow he opened his eyes and made his legs work. Somehow he staggered to a safe corner and hid himself in a hole.

"Oh my! Oh my!" thought the little dormouse. "This is dreadful! I've been wakened out of my winter sleep. Whatever shall I do? I'd better get out of this greenhouse at once before that gardener finds me and kills me."

So he crawled out of a hole in the wooden side of the greenhouse and ran into the garden.

But it was a bitterly cold winter's day, and the little dormouse felt as if he were freezing. "I shall die—I know I shall!" he said to himself, as he tried to run to and fro to keep himself warm.

Now, as he ran about, he heard a sound of crying. It was a little sound, and was rather like the leaves of trees sighing in a wind. The dormouse listened. It came from the other side of the hedge. He went through the hedge to find out what it was.

And there, curled up on the frosty grass, was a small fairy, not even as big as himself. She had on a dress made of cobwebs, and she was shivering with the cold.

"What's the matter?" asked the dormouse. "Have you been awakened from your winter sleep too?"

"No," said the fairy. "But my warm coat and my warm shawl have been taken away from me. A goblin came along and took them—and he took the blankets from my bed too, and he broke my bed to bits. It was the half of a prickly horse-chestnut case, and was so comfortable. Now I don't know what to do, for I shall freeze to death!"

"Oh no, you won't," said the dormouse, putting a

paw comfortingly round her neck. "I'll take care of you. I've been wakened from my winter sleep, and I've nowhere to go either—but we'll look after each other."

"Oh, you poor thing!" cried the little fairy. "Of course, dormice are always asleep in the winter. I quite forgot. Oh dear! You must really find a place to sleep or you will be very ill indeed. Let me help you."

Well, of course, if people help each other they soon manage to do something. The two of them began to hunt for a good place to sleep in—and whatever do you suppose they found? They found an old doll's bed belonging to the little girl who lived in the house near by. It was a very tiny bed indeed, and was very old and rusty. It had belonged to her doll's house, but because it had been left out in the rain and was rusty the little girl had thrown it away on the rubbish-heap. And there it was still, rustier than ever, with no blankets or pillows—but still, a bed.

"I really do prefer a hole of some sort to sleep in," said the dormouse.

"Well, you can't possibly find a hole in all this hard, frosty weather," said the fairy, shivering. "I do wish I could find a coat!"

They put the bed under the hedge and then they set to work to find bedclothes for it. The dormouse knew where there was some moss under the snow, for he remembered it from the summer before. So he scraped away down to it and pulled at it with his mouth. He gave the fairy quite a lot. She was delighted. She borrowed a needle from the fairy tailor, asked a hidden spider for some thread, and made herself a coat of moss and two blankets for the bed. She really was very clever with her needle.

The dormouse found some dead leaves. "They may seem dry and thin to you," he said, "but they are very warm to sleep in. Shall we have them as well in our bed?"

"Oh yes," said the fairy, and from one leaf she made herself a bonnet, and two sheets for the bed. Then the dormouse found some old thistles, still with soft thistledown in their seed-boxes. He pulled out the down and gave it the fairy. She squealed with delight.

"You really are clever at finding things," she said. "This will do to stuff the pillows and mattress with, and if there's enough I can make an eiderdown too."

There was just enough. So, very soon, there was a soft mattress on the bed, a soft pillow stuffed with thistledown, and an eiderdown made of the skin of some hips. stuffed with the down. Really, it was very gay indeed.

The sun sank. The world grew bitterly cold. The frost came creeping again over the fields, and the dormouse and the fairy shivered.

"It's time for bed," said the fairy. "Come, dormouse, and see how you sleep in a bed."

She showed him how to climb in under the blankets. Soon his little soft body was lying in bed, and his woffly nose was on the pillow. He felt warm and comfortable. The fairy climbed in beside him and cuddled up to his warm fur.

"You're as good as a hot-water bottle!" she said happily. "Oh, it's nice to help one another, isn't it? We would never have found this lovely warm bed if we hadn't made up our minds to work together and help each other. Good night, little dormouse, sleep tight!"

The dormouse was already asleep. And do you know, he is *still* asleep, for the warm days haven't yet wakened him. There he lies in the little bed—but the fairy wakes every day. She is looking for a tiny house for them to live in when he wakes up. She is going to make blue curtains for it. Won't the dormouse be surprised when he opens his eyes and sees it? Mind you don't disturb him if you find him. Just turn back the blanket and have a look at him—then cover him up warmly again, won't you?

Old Mister Glue-pot

OLD Mister Glue-Pot was a gnome who lived in Pillywee Village, on the borders of Fairyland. He kept a paint shop and sold paint in pots, and also a very sticky brown glue.

He made this glue himself, and it was so strong that just a touch of it would stick two broken pieces of a jar or dish together in a trice. Mister Glue-Pot had made a lot of money out of this very strong glue.

In fact, he had such a lot of money that he really didn't bother very much about his shop. He put Snubby, the pixie, in charge of it, and then he went into his parlour, put his feet up on the mantelpiece, and slept peacefully.

Snubby was not a good shopkeeper. He played about too much. He painted the walls of the shop green and yellow, with blue spots—and will you believe it, Mister Glue-Pot never noticed! Then Snubby discovered the glue. What a game he had with it!

First of all he got some on his hands by mistake—and, dear me, whatever Snubby touched stuck fast

to him. He touched a newspaper and that stuck. He touched two pencils and those stuck! He touched Mister Glue-Pot's best Sunday hat and that stuck. Soon you could hardly see Snubby because so many things were sticking to him!

Snubby managed to unstick himself at last. He stood looking at Mister Glue-Pot's big barrel of glue and grinned. He would have a few jokes with that!

He peeled an orange and then carefully dabbed a spot of glue on each bit of peel. When no one was looking the naughty pixie slipped out of the shop and pressed each bit of peel on the pavement. They all stuck fast. Snubby knew that Mister Plod-Plod, the policeman, would come along that way in a few minutes' time—and old Plod-Plod would certainly try to pick up all those bits of peel!

"It will be fun to see him pulling at them," giggled the naughty pixie to himself. He pressed his snubby nose against the shop window and waited. Soon he heard the plod-plod-plod noise that the policeman's feet made. Up came Mr. Plod-Plod and saw the orange peel.

"Now, who's been dropping orange peel about?" he said in his crossest voice. "It is forbidden to do such a thing!"

He looked all round but he could see no one. So Mister Plod-Plod stooped down to pick up all the bits himself—but they were stuck fast to the pavement! Plod-Plod pulled and tugged, and then stared at the peel in amazement. Was it magic? Why wouldn't it come off the pavement?

Plod-Plod took out his knife and cut all the peel away. He put it in his pocket and walked off, looking very puzzled and angry. Snubby laughed till his sides ached.

"That was a good trick!" he said. "Now what else shall I do?"

But before he could do anything else Mister Plod-Plod came back again and asked to see Mister Glue-Pot.

"Mister Glue-Pot," he said sternly, "did you

know that someone has been using your glue to stick bits of orange peel to the pavement?"

"Dear me, no!" said Glue-Pot, in a great way about it.

"Well, they have," said Plod-Plod. "Please see that you keep an eye on your glue-barrel, Glue-Pot."

"Certainly, certainly," said the old fellow, and he called Snubby to him. "Just look after the glue-barrel very carefully," he said. Snubby grinned and nodded. He would look after it all right!

Now next door to Mister Glue-Pot's shop was a baker's shop, and outside the door was a very fine mat for people to wipe their feet on. Snubby thought it would be a great joke to dab some glue on it—and then everyone's feet would get stuck there. What fun that would be!

So that night he slipped out with a brush full of glue and daubed the whole mat with it. And you should have seen the muddle there was at the baker's next day!

Dame Trit-Trot and Mister Top-hat went to the baker's shop at the same time, and both trod on the mat together. That was all right—but when they tried to walk off it into the shop they couldn't. The mat went with them! Poor Dame Trit-Trot slipped and slid, trying to get her feet off the sticky mat, and Mister Top-hat suddenly lost his balance and sat down. That was worse than ever! It took the baker two hours to untangle Trit-Trot, Top-hat, and the mat.

How angry they all were! They marched into Mister Glue-Pot's shop and banged on the counter so loudly that Mister Glue-Pot, who was fast asleep in the parlour, woke up, leapt out of his chair, and trod on his poor cat. She scratched him hard and naughty Snubby laughed till he cried.

"If you don't look after your glue better, we shall punish you, Glue-Pot!" cried Trit-Trot, Top-hat, and the baker. They told him about the sticky mat, and Glue-Pot was full of horror to think that his glue should be used for tricks like that.

"Just see you look after the glue-barrel even better than before," he said to Snubby. And Snubby grinned and said he would. But, the very next day, Snubby slipped across the road to the sweet-shop when it was empty, and dabbed the three chairs with the glue. Oh, what a dreadful thing to do!

That afternoon Snubby watched the people going in to buy sweets. He saw Mrs. Lightfoot sit down on a chair. He saw Mister Tap-tap. He saw the old brownie, Longbeard, sitting down too. They talked together for a little while till their sweets were ready—then they tried to get up to go.

But their chairs stuck to them! They ran out of the shop in horror, taking the chairs with them, though the shop-woman shouted to them to bring them back. They ran down the street with the chairs knocking behind them—and they ran straight into

Mister Plod-Plod, the policeman. And it wasn't long before he found that it was Mister Glue-Pot's glue that had done the mischief again.

He went straight to the paint-shop and shouted for Mister Glue-Pot.

"Pack up your things, take your glue and leave Pillywee Village," he ordered. "We have had enough of these glue-tricks, Mister Glue-Pot. Take this cheeky little pixie with you, for I shouldn't be surprised if he had done the mischief."

So poor Mister Glue-Pot and Snubby had to pack up and go. Snubby had to carry the barrel of glue on his back, for Mister Plod-Plod wouldn't let him leave it behind. So over the borders of Fairyland it was carried, and it's still somewhere about today.

Do you know what it is used for? Snubby and Glue-Pot sell it to the chestnut trees in the early spring, so that their buds can be painted with glue to prevent the frost from pinching them. Isn't that a good idea? Snubby paints each bud. You may see him if you look, but if you can't see him, pick a chestnut twig and feel how very strong Mister Glue-Pot's glue is. You *will* be surprised.

The Bonnet Dame

ONCE upon a time, I couldn't tell you how long ago, there lived a queer old woman, who was half a witch. She was always called the Bonnet Dame, because she got her living by making little white bonnets for babies.

Now the queer thing about Dame Bonnet was that the older she got the smaller she grew. She was thin and brown, like a bent twig, and her voice was as husky as two leaves rubbing one against the other, but her hands were still as nimble as ever, and she made her white bonnets even more beautifully.

But of course, as she grew smaller, so did the bonnets she made and after a while mothers didn't buy them any more, for they didn't fit their babies. Then Dame Bonnet went to Brownie-Town and lived there, for the brownies had nice small babies, and her bonnets fitted them well.

Then she grew smaller still and her bonnets no longer fitted even the brownie babies. So she went to Elf-land and there her bonnets fitted the grown-up elves, for they are small creatures, and when Dame Bonnet grew even smaller it didn't matter because then her lovely bonnets fitted the elf babies. So she stayed there quite a long time and was very happy indeed.

Then she grew so very small that the bonnets fitted nobody at all. She tried here and she tried there—the gnomes were far too big in the head; the goblins were the wrong shape, and even the very smallest dwarfs were too large about the head. So Dame Bonnet made no money at all, and began to shrivel away like a dead leaf.

Then one day she met some tiny creatures, slim and sweet, dressed in green. Their heads were bare,

and the wind blew their hair about untidily. Dame Bonnet looked at them and wondered if her white bonnets would fit them.

"Who are you?" she asked. "I don't think I've seen you before."

"We are the little Fair Maids," said the small creatures, "half-fairies, half-flowers. We live in the woods, and we are always trying to find a sheltered spot, because the wind blows our hair about so much. He is very rough with us, and we do not like him."

The wind swept down and whipped the tiny creatures' hair about their gentle faces. Dame Bonnet watched, and then she offered them her small white bonnets—so small now that the stitches in them could not be seen!

"Wear these!" she said, in her husky voice. "You need not pay me. Only let me keep near to you, Fair Maids, and talk to me sometimes. I am an old, old woman, and I would so much like your youthful company to cheer me."

The Fair Maids tried on the small white bonnets, and to their great delight they fitted most beautifully. "Thank you!" they said gratefully. "Please do keep near us if you like, Dame Bonnet. We shall love to talk to you."

Well, my dears, the Fair Maids still wear the tiny white bonnets made by the old half-witch. You can see them any day in February in gardens and woods, half-fairies, half-flowers—small, fairy-like snowdrops, standing in little groups together. And not far off you will perhaps see something that looks just like a shrivelled brown leaf. It *may* be a dead leaf, of course, but if it scuttles away fast when you bend down, you'll know what it really is—old Dame Bonnet herself!

Who Would Have Thought it?

FARMER GRAY was a horrid man. He had a bad temper, he was mean and nobody trusted or liked him. He got worse and worse, and at last no one would work for him. Then what a time he and his poor wife had, with the animals to feed, the stables and cowsheds to clean and any amount of other farm jobs to do!

Now one spring a little robin flew into the stable to hunt for a place to make a nest. She flew to a manger—no, that would be dangerous, for her nest might be eaten if she put it there. She flew to an old tin. Yes—that was good—but suppose it got thrown away?

She hunted all around, and at last she found a very nice place. At least, *she* thought it was. She whistled to her little mate to come and see it. He flew into the stable.

"Look," carolled the hen-robin. "Here is a place for our nest—warm, cosy, the right size and a place not likely to be seen by anyone."

Where do you suppose this place was? In the pocket of Farmer Gray's old brown coat that he had hung up on the wall and forgotten! Well, who would have thought it? The cock-robin looked at the open pocket with bright black eyes.

"Yes," he said to his mate, "it's just the place for us. That pocket will hold all the grass-roots, the leaves and the moss we use, and in this dark stable we shall be safe from weasels, stoats and jack-daws."

So they began to build their nest in the pocket of the farmer's old coat. They made a fine nest. They wove thin grass-roots together, they tucked up the holes with moss and dead leaves, and they found plenty of soft hen-feathers from the farmyard to line the nest softly.

They were very proud of it indeed. Robins always love to nest in anything belonging to humans—and this was a fine place. Soon the hen-robin laid four pretty eggs with red-brown markings. She sat on them day after day. Sometimes the cock took a turn too, so that the hen-robin might stretch her wings. He brought her many tit-bits and sometimes sang a little creamy song to her. They took no notice of the horses stamping in the stable. They got used to the hens coming in and clucking loudly. They were happy and peaceful, looking forward to the hatching of their pretty eggs.

Now one day Farmer Gray got his coat soaking wet in a rainstorm. He took it to his wife and asked her to dry it.

"Oh dear!" she said. "What are you going to wear now? Your other coat is wet too. What's become of that old brown coat you used to have?"

Farmer Grey frowned. What had he done with it? Ah—he remembered. It was in the stable, of course—it had been hanging there for months!

"It's in the stable," he said. "I'll fetch it."

Off he went. He came to the stable and looked round. "Now where's that coat of mine?" he said.

The hen-robin was sitting on her eggs in the pocket and she heard him. Her small heart beat fast in fright. Oh surely, surely Farmer Gray did not want his old coat now—just when her eggs were due to hatch at any minute! Oh no, no!

The cock-robin was perched near by. He ruffled up his feathers in fear. What! Take the coat, and crush the nest and break the eggs? Oh no, Farmer

Gray! You are a cross, rough man, and nobody likes you—but don't, don't do that!

Farmer Gray saw his coat. "Good! There it is," he said, and went over to it. The cock-robin gave a loud warble and the farmer looked round in surprise. What was the robin singing at *him* for? And then he suddenly knew the answer.

He saw the nest in the pocket of his coat as it hung on the nail. Dead leaves and bits of moss hung out of it. A small hen-robin, her red breast showing up clearly, sat in the pocket on the nest, her anxious black eyes looking trustfully at Farmer Gray.

The farmer looked down at her. He frowned and put out his hand to take the coat. And then he looked into the robin's trustful eyes, and remembered something. He remembered how, when he had been a little boy, a robin had nested in an old boot of his father's, and how delighted he had been—and how sweet the baby robins had looked about the garden. He stood and thought for a minute or two.

"Ah well, you can have my coat," he said to the little robins; "maybe you need it more than I do!" And with that he went out into the yard without a coat on.

The robins sang for joy. Farmer Gray heard them, and for the first time for years his heart was warm. It was good to be kind to another creature, even if that creature was only a robin. He saw a man going by and he called him. "Hi, John! Come and see here for a minute!"

The man came up in surprise, for it was seldom that Farmer Gray spoke nicely to anyone. The farmer took him to see the robin's nest in his old coat pocket.

"That'll bring you luck, Farmer," said John.

"I need some," said Farmer Gray. "Here's spring come along and I've no one to help me with the farm."

John looked at Farmer Gray and he thought, "Well, here's a man that everyone hates—and yet he's let the robins have his coat. He can't be so bad after all. I've a good mind to come and help him a bit."

"Well, Farmer," he said out loud, "I'll come and give you a hand when I've finished at Farmer Brown's over the hill."

Farmer Gray was pleased. He went to the farm and told his wife about the robins and about how John was going to work for him.

"Those robins will bring me luck," he said, and he laughed. His wife was glad. She had been lonely without any friends to speak to.

John came. He worked hard. He got another man to come. Everything went well. The robins hatched out their eggs, and baby robins fluttered in the old stable. Farmer Gray brought them meal-worms and they grew so tame that they would fly on to his shoulders. How proud Farmer Gray was then! He called all sorts of people in to see his tame robins—

and that meant giving them something to eat and drink and maybe a cigarette. Soon the farmer had plenty of friends, and he forgot to frown and grumble.

"Here, wife. Here's money to buy you a new dress and a new hat," said Farmer Gray. "We're making money. Things are better. We've got friends to help us. My word! Those robins have brought me luck all right."

"It wasn't really the robins," said his wife. "It was the bit of kindness in your heart, William, that made you spare the robins and their nest. If you had not had that bit of kindness, you would have had no good luck!"

And she was right, wasn't she? We make our own good luck, there's no doubt about that!

Black Boot Buttons

ONE day Betty and Fred had such a funny adventure. They were going home from school over the fields when they heard someone saying something over and over again.

"Oh dear, oh dear, oh dear, oh dear, oh dear!" said somebody. And then he started off again: "Oh dear, oh dear, oh dear, oh dear, oh dear!"

"Whoever can that be?" wondered Betty. "It's someone on the other side of the hedge, Fred. Let's look, shall we?"

So they squeezed through a hole in the hedge and looked. And on the other side they saw a strange sight.

A small man sat in the grass. He had on a tall, pointed hat set with little bells. He wore a green tunic and long black stockings, and on his legs were high button boots—with no buttons on! The children stared in surprise.

"Oh dear, oh dear, oh dear, oh dear, oh dear!" began the little man again—and then he caught sight of the children.

"Oh dear, oh..." he began, but Betty stopped him.

"Please don't say it again or we shall laugh!" she said. "What's the matter?"

"Look at my boots," said the little man. "I was on my way to visit my brother, Sir Up-and-Down, who lives in the wood yonder, in a very nice oak-tree. I sat down here to rest a little and fell asleep. When I awoke I found that a mischievous pixie had been along and cut all the buttons off my button boots.

He has taken them with him too—and now, here am I, on my way to visit Sir Up-and-Down, and haven't even a button on my boots!"

The children stared. They knew they must be talking to someone belonging to the fairies. But he didn't look like a fairy. He was very upset about his boots.

"Oh dear, oh dear, oh dear, oh..." he began again, and Betty and Fred laughed. It did sound so funny.

"Don't laugh. It's rude," said the little man crossly. "You should help people when they are in trouble, not laugh at them."

"Well, we would like to help you," said Betty. "But I don't see how we can. We don't wear button boots or shoes, only laced ones. We have no buttons to give you, and the village shop is two miles away. It would take too long to go there and back. Besides, today is early-closing day."

"Just my luck," said the little man gloomily. "If only I could find some buttons. I could put them on in a trice then, and go to visit my brother."

He got up and looked down at his boot. He shook his head and began to walk off slowly. "Oh dear, oh dear, oh dear, oh dear, oh dear!" the children heard him say as he went.

They watched him go, and then they turned to walk home. They felt excited to have met such a strange little man, who had a brother with such a funny name, living in such a queer place.

Now as they went on their way they came to a thick ivy hedge—and on it, growing in big clusters, were berries as round and as black as boot-buttons. Fred saw them first and stopped with a shout.

"Betty, look! The ivy has berries just like boot-buttons. Do you suppose they would do for the little man? If he belongs to the fairies he may know some magic and could sew them on his boots quite easily."

"Let's run back and tell him," said Betty. So the two children ran back down the path, calling loudly: "Little man, little man, stop!"

The little fellow had not gone very far. He

stopped and ran back to the children.

"What is it?" he cried. "Have you got some black boot-buttons for me?"

"Yes" said Betty. "Come and look!"

She led him to the ivy hedge, and the little man gazed at the clusters of black berries there.

"The very thing," he said. "Pick me some, please."

Betty and Fred picked him a big bunch. He took the biggest and blackest berries, doubled the stalks of each one over to make a loop, and took a needle and cotton from a case in his pocket.

He sat down. He muttered a magic word to the needle, and to the children's great astonishment it began to sew on those ivy-buttons as quick as could be. In half a minute the little man's boots had a row of buttons on each one. He buttoned them up and beamed at the children.

"Just the very thing," he said. "Why didn't I think of it myself? Thank you, children. Is there anything I can do for you in return?"

"Do you think you could manage to let us have a kitten of our own?" asked Betty in excitement. "We've always wanted one, but we've never had one."

"Oh yes, I'll manage that easily," said the little man. "Look on your doorstep tomorrow morning. Good-bye now, I'm off to see my brother."

He ran off and the children went home in great excitement—and will you believe it, when they opened the door next morning there on the door-step they found a dear little kitten, with fur as black as the ivy berries! They called it Ivy, of course, and it still lives with them, though now it has grown into an enormous black cat with green eyes. Betty is sure it came from a witch.

Would you like to see some of the black boot-buttons that the little man sewed on to his boots? Then go and look at the berries in the ivy now, and you will see some. They are round and black—just like boot-buttons! You will be so pleased with them.

The Tom Thumb Fairies

ONCE upon a time there were some very small creatures called Tom Thumb fairies—so small that you could easily hold a hundred in the palm of your hand and hardly feel any weight.

They lived in some little red toadstools in Toadstool Village on the borders of Fairyland. The toadstools were small enough, goodness knows, but the fairies were so tiny that each toadstool was as big as a house to them. So they hung curtains at the windows in the top, and had a little door in the stalk with a knocker and a letter-box, just as you have.

Now one night there came a band of red goblins creeping round Toadstool Village. It was a dark night and there were so many clouds that not even the stars gave their faint light. The goblin chief gave a signal, and at once two goblins went to each toadstool house, opened the door and captured the small fairy inside the bedroom at the top of the toadstool.

Nobody heard them squeal. Nobody heard them

struggle. They were popped into bags and taken off to Goblin Town at once, there to wait on the goblins and help them with their spells. Their wings were clipped off, so that they could not fly home. The wings grew again in a few weeks' time, but every time they grew the goblins clipped them off again.

The Tom Thumb fairies were very unhappy. "What shall we do?" they wept. "We hate working underground all day long. We hate these red goblins, who are so unkind. We don't know the way home. We have no wings to fly with."

One day one of the Tom Thumb fairies found a worm-hole leading up to the sunlight. She was over-joyed, and she whispered the news to the others.

"One morning when the goblins have gone off somewhere, we will creep up this worm-hole and escape," said the fairy.

"But the goblins will come after us," said the others. "We shan't know which way to go when we get up into daylight again."

"Never mind," said the first one. "We will see what we can do."

So the next time the red goblins went off together, leaving the Tom Thumb fairies to do all the work, the tiny creatures began to make their way up the worm-hole. It was very small—but they were smaller still.

Soon they came to the worm, and they could not get by, for the worm was fat and lay squeezed up in its bedroom—a large part of the hole halfway down the passage.

"Please move up a bit," said one of the Tom Thumbs, poking the worm. "We want to get by."

The worm moved up its hole. It put out its head and listened, for it had no eyes to see with. Was any sharp-eyed bird about? No—it could hear no pattering of feet. So it drew itself right up and let the fairies use its rather slimy hole as a passage up to the daylight.

How pleased the Tom Thumbs were when they saw the bright sunshine again! "Now we must plan what to do," they cried.

"Get back into your hole," shouted a fairy to the worm. "The red goblins may come after us. Don't you move out of your hole for them, or they will catch us."

"There are plenty of other holes for the red goblins to come up by," said the worm, sliding back again. "There's the mouse-hole just over there—and the big rabbit-hole in the hedge—and any amount of empty worm-holes too."

"Oh dear!" said the Tom Thumbs, looking round as if they expected to see the red goblins at any moment. "We had better find a hiding-place in case they come. Where can we go?"

There were pink-tipped daises about—much, much bigger than the Tom Thumb fairies. There was a large dandelion plant too, with great golden blossoms.

"I will hide you," said the dandelion in a soft silky

voice. "You are so tiny that you can each slip under one of my many golden petals. Hurry now, for I can hear the red goblins coming."

In a trice the Tom Thumbs had run to the large dandelion, which spread its hundreds of soft petals to the sun. Each fairy lifted up a silken petal and slipped underneath. There they hid in safety whilst the red goblins, suddenly appearing from the mouse-hole, began to hunt for the Tom Thumbs.

"They must be somewhere about," shouted the chief one. "Hunt well, all of you."

Well, they hunted and they hunted, but no one thought of looking in the dandelion-head. There the Tom Thumbs hid, and did not make a movement for fear of being found.

"Well, goblins, we must get back to our home underground," said the chief at last. "But you, Gobo, and you, Feefo, and you, Huggo, stay up here and keep watch in case those Tom Thumbs are hiding anywhere."

The goblins went back down the mouse-hole, but Gobo, Feefo and Huggo stayed behind, their sharp black eyes looking round and about. The Tom Thumbs did not dare to move.

"Don't worry," whispered the dandelion. "You have a soft bed—and if you look hard you will find honey to eat, and when the night comes you will have dew to drink. Keep still and rest, and you will be safe."

Day after day the Tom Thumbs lay hidden in the

golden dandelion, whilst the three goblins kept a strict watch. The dandelion grew on its stalk and lifted the Tom Thumbs higher—and then something queer happened.

It was time for the golden dandelion-head to fade. The gold left it—it closed up like a bud once more, holding the Tom Thumbs safely inside. It was no longer a wide golden flower, but a rather untidy-looking dead one, tightly shut. It drooped its head so low that it hid it amongst the leaves. Still the Tom Thumbs lay hidden—because now they could not get out!

What would happen to them? They did not know. The honey was almost finished, and the dew no longer fell on to them for drink. They huddled together in the dead flower, frightened and miserable.

The stalk of the dandelion grew longer and longer. How queer! But it had a reason. Yes—for the flower was turning into seed—and when that seed was ready it must be taken up into the air on a long, long stalk so that the wind might blow it away. Oh, clever dandelion!

So it came about that one day the dead dandelion raised its head again, on its long, long stalk. It stood straight up once more, and—wonder of wonders!—instead of a golden head it now had a head full of marvellous white seeds. It was a beautiful dandelion clock.

And now the Tom Thumb fairies began to get

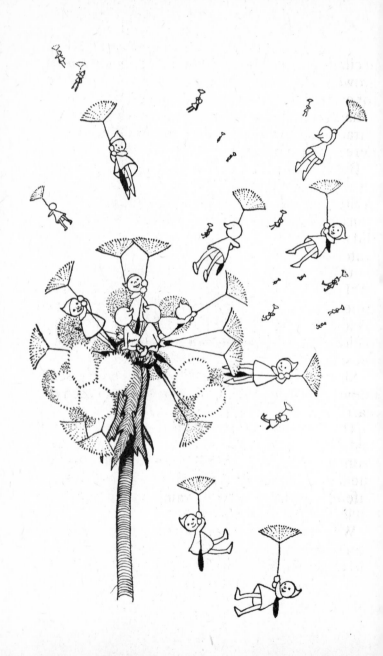

excited. "Look!" they cried. "The dandelion has grown us little parachutes! Do look! There is one for each of us. We can hold on to the stalk—it is like a handle for us—and when the wind blows, the parachute of hairs will carry us far, far away from here, safe from the red goblins."

But the wind did not blow them away—someone else did. Who was that? Well, it may have been you! A little girl came down that way and saw the dandelion clock standing there, so tall and beautiful. She did not see the three red goblins still keeping a sharp watch. She picked the dandelion clock and looked at it.

"I shall blow you," she said. "I want to know the time. Now then—PUFF!—one o'clock. PUFF!—two o'clock. PUFF!—three o'clock. PUFF!—four o'clock. PUFF!—five o'clock. Oh, it's tea-time! I must hurry."

She ran off, pleased to see the pretty seeds blowing in the air—but she didn't see that each one carried a Tom Thumb fairy.

The dandelion seeds flew high and far. When at last they came to the ground they were far, far away from the red goblins' home. The Tom Thumbs took the first bus home they could find; and now they are safe in Toadstool Village again—and at night they all lock and bolt their doors!

Wasn't it lucky for them that they hid in a dandelion? And what a lovely ride they had when the little girl puffed the clock away!

Andrew's Robin

IN Andrew's garden there was a robin that he called his own. It was a black-eyed, long-legged, red-breasted little bird, so tame that it would take a bit of biscuit from Andrew's fingers.

That summer the robin had built its nest in an old saucepan under the hedge. Andrew remembered

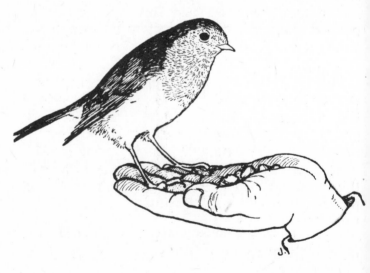

putting the saucepan there when he played house, and he had forgotten to take it away. The robin found it, and he and his little wife had put a cosy nest there.

Andrew was pleased. He watched the robins going to and from the nest. He saw the five eggs they laid there. He even saw three of the eggs hatch out. That *was* exciting. The tiny birds inside the eggs pecked at the shell and broke it. Then out they came—bare black babies without a single feather on them.

The next day all five eggs had hatched. The robins threw the empty shells out of the saucepan nest, and began hunting for caterpillars and grubs to feed their five hungry babies.

"That will keep you busy," said Andrew, as he peeped at the five tiny birds, all with their beaks wide open. "When I dig my garden I will hunt for caterpillars too, and bring them to you."

One day a dreadful thing happened to the robins. A grey squirrel came that way and saw the nest in the saucepan. Now the grey squirrel liked, for a change, to make a meal of baby birds, so when he saw the little robins he ran over to them at once.

The father and mother robin were not there, as they had gone hunting for grubs. The squirrel picked up two of the tiny creatures in his mouth and ran off with them.

How those babies squeaked! The father and mother robin heard them at once and came flying back. When they saw the grey squirrel they knew quite well what he had been up to, and they flew at him, singing loudly in anger, for that is the way of robins.

The squirrel stopped. One robin flew at his right eye and the other flew at his left. He shook his head. He dodged. But it was no use. Those robins would not leave him alone until he dropped the baby birds.

So the grey squirrel dropped them on the lawn, and then bounded off to a tree. Up he went and sat there making faces at the robins.

The robins flew down to their two frightened babies. They were not really hurt—but they could not possibly get back to the nest themselves.

"We must carry them in our beaks," sang the mother robin. But alas! the babies were too heavy.

"Leave them, leave them!" sang the freckled thrush. "I don't bother about my young ones if they fall from the nest."

But the robins were not like the thrush. They would not leave their little ones. But what could they do? The babies were too heavy to carry.

"Fetch Andrew, fetch Andrew!" sang the father robin. "He is kind and strong."

So the robins went to fetch Andrew. He was in the nursery, building a big castle, and was very surprised to see the two robins fly in at the window. The rather robin flew to the top of Andrew's big castle and sang loudly to him. Andrew stared at him. The robin flew to the window and back again.

"What is it you want?" asked Andrew, puzzled. The robin sang again and flew to the window-sill. Andrew got up and went too—and he saw something on the lawn. What could it be?

He ran downstairs and out into the garden. As soon as he came to the baby birds, lying helpless on the grass, he guessed why the robins had come to him.

"They want me to put their babies back," said Andrew in delight. "Oh, the clever little things! They knew I would help them."

He gently lifted the two frightened baby birds and took them to the nest in the saucepan. He put them with the others and they soon settled down happily.

"Thank you!" sang the robins. "You are kind!"

The robins were afraid of the squirrel after that. Always one of them stayed to guard the nest until the babies were too big to be taken away by a squirrel. Soon they could fly. Soon they had flown. The little robin family split up, and they all left the garden, except the father robin. This little bird stayed there with Andrew, singing to him as he played in the garden. He never once forgot how kind the little boy had been to the baby birds.

One day Andrew took his clockwork train and lines on to the lawn. He set the train going and had a wonderful time with it. When it was tea-time he had to pack it up in a hurry and go in, and it wasn't till the next day that he found he had lost the key of his beautiful clockwork engine.

"Oh, Mummy, now I can't play with my engine any more, because the key is lost," he said. "I have hunted everywhere in the garden, but I can't find it. I am so unhappy."

The robin heard him. He had seen Andrew winding up the engine. He guessed what the key was— that little shiny thing. He began to hunt for it.

And at last he found it. No wonder Andrew couldn't see it, for it was halfway down a worm's burrow. The robin pulled it out. It was a bit rusty, but it was the lost key, no doubt about that.

The robin took it in his beak and flew to the nursery. He sat on the window-sill and made a little creamy sound, for he couldn't sing very loudly with something in his beak. Andrew looked up.

"Oh!" he cried in great delight. "You've found my key! You dear, good little bird! Thank you so much!"

"You helped me, and I helped you!" carolled the robin. "That is as it should be. Soon it will be winter-time, Andrew. Help me again and give me crumbs."

"I will, I will!" promised Andrew. And I know he will keep his promise.

Would You Believe It?

REDDY, the stickleback, was a very lively little fish. He swam about the pond, and everyone there knew him very well.

The tadpoles knew him and kept out of his way, because he had sharp spines along his back and tried to prick them if they were rude to him.

The big black beetles knew him too, and often talked to him. The grubs at the bottom, in the mud, told him all their news, and the minnows (fish as small as he was) liked to have him swim with them.

The stickleback was afraid of nothing and nobody. He didn't even mind the big, fierce dragon-fly grub who hid in the mud, and flashed out big pincers to catch his dinner. Reddy was far too quick for him.

He was called Reddy because he had a very hot temper, and when he lost his temper the little fish turned a bright red. Everyone knew when the stickleback was angry. The tadpoles fled away to the other side of the pond then. "Danger! Danger!" they would say to one another. "Reddy's gone scarlet with rage. Red for danger!"

Now one day in the spring, Reddy saw a tiny fly on the surface of the water, just at the edge of the pond. He swam up to catch it—and dear me, he almost got pecked by a small sparrow who was just dipping in her beak to have a sip of water. He backed away in alarm, and went scarlet with rage.

The sparrow peered into the water in surprise. She had never seen a fish go red before. "Come up here!" she chirped. "You're pretty when you go red like that. I won't hurt you. I was only sipping the water. I don't eat fish, so you are quite safe."

Reddy was always pleased to talk to somebody new, so he swam near. He rather liked the look of the little brown sparrow. She was cheeky and lively—and so was he!

"Do *you* go red when you're angry?" he asked. "I once saw a bird with a very red breast. Was it you?"

"Oh no, that was the robin," said the sparrow. "He always has a red breast, not because he's cross, but just as a danger signal. Red things usually taste nasty. I never turn red, I'm afraid. I'm always this rather dull brown."

The two stayed and talked for a long time. The sparrow wanted Reddy to come out of the water, but he said he couldn't; he would die.

"You come down into the pond," he said. "I could show you a lot of things here."

"No, I couldn't breathe down there," said the sparrow. "I should have to grow gills and fins and scales to live with you—and you'd have to grow feathers to fly in the air with me. We're too different to live together—but it would be nice to be friends."

"Yes. You come down and talk to me each day,"

said the stickleback. So each morning the sparrow flew down for a drink and a chat, and the stickleback and bird told all their little bits of news.

"I've got four eggs," said the sparrow one day. "How many have you got?"

"None," said the stickleback, and he began to go red with anger. "As soon as I find a wife and get her to lay some eggs for me in the weeds, a beetle or a tadpole comes along, finds them and eats them. I can't keep my eggs safe at all."

"What a pity," said the sparrow. "Mine are nice and safe. Soon they will hatch out into tiny birds and I shall be very happy then."

"How do you keep your eggs safe from other creatures?" asked the stickleback.

"I build a nest for them," said the sparrow. "You should do the same, stickleback."

"What's a nest?" said the little fish. "I've never seen one."

"Oh, it's a cosy little home made of anything you can find," said the sparrow. "I make mine of leaves and straw and hay and feathers—all packed together, you know—and inside I put my eggs. Then I sit on them and guard them, and I look after my babies when they hatch out."

"Sparrow, that's the best idea I ever heard of!" said the tiny fish, and he went red with excitement. "Do you think I could make a nest for *my* eggs?"

"Why not?" said the sparrow. "There are all kinds of bits floating about in the water. You could collect them together and make a dear little nest. Then you could make your wife lay her eggs there, and you could keep guard on them all day long yourself."

"I'll go and begin this very minute," said Reddy, still scarlet with excitement. Off he swam, and began to collect all kinds of bits—pieces of water-weed, bits of decayed stuff, straw, anything he could stick together to make a nest.

Now, he had never seen a bird's nest. He didn't know the right cup-shape, as most birds do, and he made it more like a muff. But he thought it was quite the right shape, and he worked very hard indeed to finish it.

All the other creatures swam round in astonishment. "What's that? A house to live in?" asked the minnows.

"No, a nest for my eggs," said Reddy.

"A *nest*?" said the minnows. "You must be mad; or maybe you think you're a bird, Reddy."

"Go away," cried Reddy, and he swam at them, his spines looking so sharp that the minnows shot off in fright.

The tadpoles came nosing round. A big black beetle actually swam right through the muff-like nest, and Reddy was so angry that he chased him round the pond, and gave the poor beetle such a fright that he went up to the surface, climbed on to a stick, spread his wings and flew off. Reddy was astonished. He had forgotten that the water-beetle

JOYCE
JOHNSON

could fly!

"Now I must look for a wife who will lay me some eggs in my beautiful nest," said Reddy, and he swam off to find one. He soon found one and chased her to the nest. She liked it. She went in and laid a few tiny eggs. Reddy went in to have a look at them.

"Lay some more!" he cried, and swam after her. "You haven't laid me enough."

But she swam away and wouldn't lay any more. So Reddy had to find another wife and ask her to lay more eggs for him.

Soon he had enough. He was very proud of them. The only time he left them was when he swam off once to tell the sparrow that he too had a nest. He described it to the little bird and she chirruped with laughter.

"You haven't made it right. It shouldn't be that shape at all."

"It's the very best shape," said Reddy crossly. "It's just right for my eggs."

After that he didn't leave his eggs at all. Now that everyone in the pond knew where they were he had to guard them well. He swam about near the nest and chased away anyone who came to peep. He was nearly always red with rage those days!

The tadpoles came to peep. The water-spider dropped down to have a look. The caddis-grubs crawled up to see. The big dragon-fly came too, but Reddy wouldn't let him even see his eggs.

"I know you, with your nasty pincers," he said.

"Go away! You would eat all my eggs if I left them for a moment."

The sun was hot on the water, and the pond grew very warm. Reddy went near his nest of eggs and fanned the water quickly with his fins and tail. Then he nosed the eggs about a little and spread them out. What dear little eggs they were! They would soon hatch out now.

There was no one but Reddy to guard the nest. His little wives didn't come near it. They didn't seem to mind what happened to their eggs at all. But Reddy did. He loved them. He knew what the sparrow felt now, when she looked at her eggs and wished they would hatch.

And then one day his eggs did hatch—not into tiny birds, but into very, very tiny fish. Reddy was beside himself with joy, and he went bright scarlet with delight and excitement. He told everyone his news.

"My eggs have hatched out. They are tiny fish now. I have a family of my own!"

The news soon went round the pond. "We will make a nice meal of those baby fish as soon as they swim out of that silly nest," said the tadpoles.

"I'll nip those little fish when they swim by me," said the dragon-fly.

But Reddy wasn't going to let the tiny fish out of his sight. They had to stay in the nest till they were able to swim quite quickly. He pulled the top part of the nest away to give them room, and then, later on, he let them out to swim.

"You're to keep with me," he told them, "and at the least sign of danger I shall chase you back to the nest. If any of you disobeys I shall run my stickles into him."

But he didn't need to do that, for the tiny fish were good and obedient. They swam beside their father, and if he saw the dragon-fly grub coming along he would head them all back to the nest. Back they would go and lie there peacefully till he told them they could come out once more.

One day they were quite well-grown, and Reddy knew it was time for them to look after themselves. He had shown them all their enemies; he had warned them of any dangers in the pond; he had taught them how to feed themselves. Now they must grow up and go their own way in the pond.

"But first of all come and see my friend, the sparrow," he said. "She will like to see you. I think I heard her chirruping just now, over there at the edge of the pond."

The stickleback took his little brood of fish along with him, their tiny spines sticking up just like his— and there, at the edge of the water, showing her little family how to drink, was the sparrow.

"I've brought my family to see you," said the stickleback proudly. "Look at them! I want to thank you for telling me how to make a nest for my eggs. The others all laughed at me—but it was a wonderful idea, because now I have hatched out all my eggs, and have brought up my own family!"

"And here is *my* little family," said the sparrow proudly. "Four of them. All my eggs hatched out safely. The baby birds are just growing up, and will soon be ready to fly off on their own."

"When they've done that and you haven't got to look after them any more, come down to the water each day and talk to me, as you used to do," said the stickleback.

The sparrow promised that she would. Then she and her little brown family flew off.

The stickleback swam away from his children. He knew it was time for them to look after themselves.

"I shall often see you," he said. "And remember, when spring-time comes again, do as I did—build yourselves little nests for your eggs. Then you will be as happy as I am."

From that time on all sticklebacks have made nests for their eggs. What a strange thing for fish to do! If you don't believe me, get two little stickle-backs for yourself, and put them into an aquarium.

They will build a nest, and put their eggs there— and you can watch for yourself all that happens.